THE MEMORY HORSE

TROON HARRISON
Illustrated by EUGENIE FERNANDES

Tundra Books

Published in Canada by Tundra Books, *McClelland & Stewart Young Readers*,
481 University Avenue, Toronto, Ontario M5G 2E9

Published in the United States by Tundra Books of Northern New York,
P.O. Box 1030, Plattsburgh, New York 12901

Library of Congress Catalog Number: 99-70966

Canadian Cataloguing in Publication Data
Harrison, Troon, 1958-
        The memory horse

ISBN 0-88776-440-1

I. Fernandes, Eugenie. II. Title.

PS8565.A6587M45 1999   jC813'.54   C99-930629-4
PZ7.H37Me 1999

We acknowledge the support of the Canada Council for the Arts and
the Ontario Arts Council for our publishing program.

We acknowledge the financial support of the Government of Canada through
the Book Publishing Industry Development Program for our publishing activities.
Canadä

Design by Ingrid Paulson

Printed and bound in Canada

1 2 3 4 5 6   04 03 02 01 00 99

When we moved to Grandpa's farm, I asked him to show me around. Together we walked over the fields to the village.

In the fairground, the carousel was faded and silent. My grandpa looked sad as he ran a hand over the horses' chipped paint. "Your grandmother used to love this carousel," he told me. "At your age, she would ride it all afternoon when the county fair was on. She would hate to see it looking like this."

I wished that she could see it anyway – that she hadn't died.

I wished that I could swoop around on shining horses, while music played and wind blew through my hair.

"Have you heard about the carousel?" my mother asked at supper one evening. "In the village, people are saying it should be saved. There's a plan for each family to adopt a horse and pay for it to be restored."

"Who cares about that old thing?" said my brother. "I'd rather have a hockey rink."

"That carousel is part of village history," said my father, "and I'm sorry I have no money to spare. I still have to pay the vet's bill and get that baler fixed before haying time. No use asking me for money."

"I wish there was something we could do to help!" I said unhappily, but then Grandpa winked at me.

When Grandpa and I reached the fairground, it was packed with trucks and cars. People had come for miles to adopt a carousel horse. I dragged at Grandpa's hand. "Hurry, hurry! There will be no horses left," I said, but he walked slowly all around the carousel, peering over shoulders.

"There it is," he said. "There's the horse your grandma loved best. She called it Starflyer."

"Can we adopt it, Grandpa? Please let's do it for Grandma."

"I'll see how much it costs," he said. "Can't make you any promises."

A long line of people waited to pay for a horse. I was sure that we would be too late to get any horse at all, and I wanted us to have Starflyer. But, perhaps it would cost too much money.

While Grandpa stood in line, I went and talked to my friend Sally. We waited for a long time. At last Grandpa came to find me.

"Did you get Starflyer?" I asked breathlessly. "Did you, Grandpa?"

"Yes," he replied. "I've paid the money for Starflyer to be repaired."

I was so happy I gave Grandpa a bear hug.

"You'll break my ribs," he teased.

When the men arrived to work on the carousel, Grandpa and I went to watch. First, they took it all apart. After the horses were sanded smooth, and had any cracks or holes filled in, they would be painted beautiful colors. Each one would be different.

"I wish we could do Starflyer ourselves, Grandpa. I wish you could paint it," I said.

"Oh, I'm not a good enough artist to do that." Grandpa chuckled, but he was wrong. Since my family had taken over the farm work, Grandpa had painted many beautiful things.

"Some people may have thought your grandma was real ordinary," Grandpa told me when we got home, "but I'm going to tell you a story to show how special she was."

I snuggled down in the cushions and waited for Grandpa's story.

"Your grandma was a woman who worked hard, but the best thing about her was how much she liked to help people. When the war was on, she got real sad, seeing all those young people getting on the train and going away across the ocean to fight.

"She started writing letters to them. She wrote hundreds of letters to soldiers, telling them how she was thinking about them when they were so far from home. She wrote at night, after working all day on the farm. I used to fall asleep, watching her.

"One day she got word that one of the soldiers she wrote to had been sent back wounded. Your grandma caught the train and went to visit him. He was lying in a hospital bed, looking thin and white and scared of life. Your grandma said it hurt her just to see him.

"Though he was a stranger, she got him all packed up and brought him home to our farm. We put him in a room with the windows open, so he could smell the fresh cut hay. She fed him eggs from our own chickens, and fresh farm milk. She made him rhubarb pies and raspberry ice cream, and pretty soon that soldier began to get better. His wounds healed, and he had a smile on his face again."

"Then what, Grandpa?" I asked. "Did he go back to the war?"

"Nope," said Grandpa. "He never went back again. He's a man you know real well."

"I do?" I asked. How could I know a soldier who Grandma rescued before I was even born?

"He's your dad," Grandpa said. "That soldier stayed to help us on the farm. He married our daughter Jeannie, who's your mom."

At night I sat in bed and remembered Grandma, who had saved my dad. Without her kindness I would not have been born. I wanted to do something to remember Grandma, to show other people that she was a very special person. Then I had an idea about her favorite carousel horse.

In the morning I told Grandpa my idea. At first he wouldn't agree to what I wanted, but I kept asking him. I asked him every morning and every evening before bed and, finally, he agreed.

The village let Grandpa bring Starflyer home in his truck. Grandpa began to paint the horse while I watched. He worked on it for weeks.

He painted speckled hens and ears of corn and raspberries. This was to help us remember how hard Grandma had worked on the farm – how she had planted and hoed in the garden, how she had made jam and pies.

The ribbons were those that Grandma had won at the county fair for her pickles and pumpkins.

Grandpa painted scraps of bright fabric, like the pieces Grandma used to sew quilts. He said her stitches were tiny and straight.

*H*e painted a moose, like the one she had skinned out one winter, when she and Grandpa were very poor. She made Grandpa a beautiful coat from the moose hide – it kept him warm for many years.

The baby raccoons were a family that Grandma had saved after the dog got their mother. She fed them from a bottle.

Grandpa painted stamps to remember all those hundreds of letters my grandma had written late at night to homesick soldiers.

The train was to remember how Grandma brought the sick soldier home, before he was my dad. The cow was to remember all the fresh milk she had carried up the stairs, trying to make the soldier strong again.

The star on the horse's forehead was to remember how Grandma called it Starflyer.

*T*he apple blossom was to remember a wedding in the farm orchard, when the soldier married Grandma's daughter, who is my mom.

Last of all Grandpa painted a beautiful heart, and inside it he wrote Grandma's name: *Anna*. This was to celebrate how much we loved her.

When all the horses were repaired and painted, they were fastened back onto the carousel. The village held a special celebration, and people came for miles to ride the horses. Their paint was shiny and their eyes were bright. Their brass poles gleamed. Music played. Children laughed. My brother could hardly wait for his turn to climb on the carousel. My friend Sally said she was going to ride once on every horse. There was only one horse that I wanted to ride.

$\mathcal{I}$ rode the memory horse all afternoon, while wind blew through my hair. Around and around the memory horse soared, high above the crowd. I felt like I was flying. Grandpa waved every time I swooped past. He said that I looked just like Grandma had, riding at the county fair when she was young.